Sid the Mosquito
and Other Wild Stories

'Sid's mouth was filled with a million
wonderful tastes. The pollen tasted
like strawberry jam, caramel pudding
and black cherry ice-cream. The
nectar was like thick chocolate sauce
and creme eggs floating in condensed
milk. Of course, Sid was only a little
mosquito and had never heard of
chocolate or all the other delicious
things. All he knew was that what he
was eating was totally amazingly
completely fantastic and he was
feeling sick.'

Twelve wild stories from a garden.

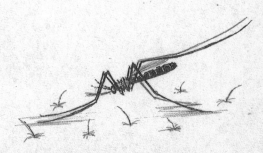

Sid the Mosquito and Other Wild Stories

Colin Thompson

Illustrations by the author

Hodder
Children's
Books

a division of Hodder Headline plc

First published in Great Britain in 1993
by Knight Books

A Catalogue record for this book is available from the British
Library

ISBN 0-340-59290 7

Typeset by Hewer Text Composition Services, Edinburgh.

Printed and bound in Great Britain
by Cox & Wyman Ltd, Reading, Berks.

Hodder Children's Books
A Division of Hodder Headline plc
338 Euston Road
London NW1 3BH

Contents

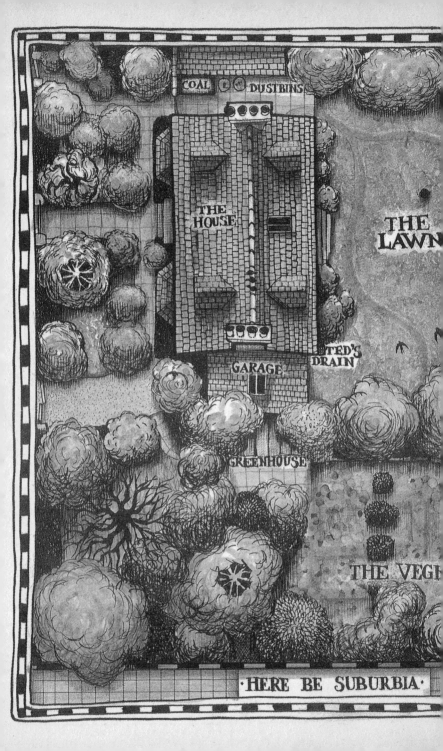

This book is dedicated
to the memory of
Margery Fisher,
1913–1992,
who was so kind to Ethel.

Going to Sleep

At the end of a quiet street, at the edge of a large town, stood a beautiful old house. The honeysuckle grew high around its walls and the paint curled up at the edges of the windows. Behind the dusty glass, dark velvet curtains brushed against a forest of cobwebs and at the back of the house a wide lawn led down to a tangle of fruit trees and a forgotten pond.

At the top of the street the traffic hurried by but in this short road that led to nowhere it was peaceful and quiet.

Around the house and lawn, tall trees and thick bushes grew wonderful and wild with birds and creatures and insects that flashed in the flickering sunlight. Hedgehogs slipped beneath overgrown branches, watched from the cellar windows by dark brown rats. Mosquitos hovered over the lawn in the misty haze of summer and from beneath the eaves of the house swallows swooped down to catch them. At the bottom of the garden there were rabbits and in the tops of the trees there were squirrels.

An old lady and an old dog lived in the house. The old lady had been born there when the house had been bright and new and full of people. With her brothers and sisters she had run through the rooms and every corner of the house had been full of sunshine and laughter.

Everyone else was gone now. Her mother and father had died a long time ago and her brothers and sisters all lived far away in other towns.

She had lived all her life in the house. They had grown old together. Twelve years ago, her nephew, who thought she might be lonely, had bought her the dog. For the first time in her long life the old lady had someone who needed her. And for the first time in years the house was filled with words as she talked to her new friend.

'Shall we go and pick some flowers?' she would say, or, 'Time for a cup of tea, I think.'

Every morning the old lady opened the back door and the old dog shuffled out into the garden. He sniffed the dustbin, lifted his face to the sky to catch the smells of the day and then set off round his territory.

'Morning,' said the weasels as he passed their hole in the wall.

'Morning,' said the dog as he ambled by.

'Nice day,' said the mole.

'It's raining,' said the dog.

'Yes, but it's nice rain.'

The dog was always surprised to see the mole. No matter what time of day he went round the garden, she would be there, just coming out of her hole. What he didn't know was that she was lonely and listened for his footsteps across the lawn. She thought he was wonderful and as he walked across the grass she scampered beneath him down her tunnels so that she could pop up as he went by.

'Morning,' said the dog to the old chicken who lived in a box at the bottom of the lawn. The chicken was even older than he was and when he went by she was usually fast asleep and didn't answer.

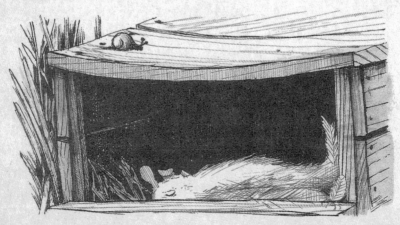

As he passed the dark wooden shed where the lawnmower and the deck-chairs were kept, he pushed his nose into the hole where the hedgehogs lived.

'It's raining,' he said into the dark space under the shed. His daily weather report was usually met with sleepy grunts. Most of the hedgehogs slept all day, particularly if it was raining. Some of the young ones were often about, snuffling in the dandelions for slugs, but it was very rare to see an adult hedgehog before mid-afternoon.

The dog moved on to the bottom of the garden where there was a rusty car that had once taken the old lady to school. Now it was full of ferns and mice who lived behind the dashboard.

'I do wish he wouldn't do that,' they said when the dog lifted his leg against the front tyre.

'I know,' said a sparrow who had built her nest in the glove compartment. 'It lowers the tone of the whole neighbourhood.'

As the dog walked under the tall sycamore trees, the crows that nested high up in the top branches called down to him.

'Good morning, dog,' they cried.

'What? Who said that?' said the dog, looking round. It was the same every day. He never thought of looking up towards the sky and he had begun to believe the trees were haunted. The crows thought the dog was stupid and shouted to him each day as a joke.

Past the car was the rabbit warren. The dog didn't know what to make of the rabbits. He was a gentle, quiet animal and the rabbits were loud and rough, not at all like rabbits are supposed to be. Large eyes peered out of the holes as he went by. Rabbits are supposed to be frightened of dogs but these laughed and whistled and he kept away from them.

He ambled through the orchard, sometimes eating a fallen apple, before coming out on to the lawn again and wandering up to the back door where he sat and barked until the old lady let him in.

On summer days the old lady opened the French windows at the back of the house and the dog came out to lie in the sunshine. He lay in the middle of the lawn and got hotter and hotter until he was panting like a steam train. Then he would go to the pond for a drink and come back to lie under the bushes.

'You know,' he said to a hedgehog as they lay together under a gooseberry bush, 'My human's amazing. I'd swear she understands my every thought.' Across the lawn, the old lady was sitting by the open door knitting a blue blanket.

'Yes,' agreed the hedgehog. 'She's almost dog-like.'

'You're absolutely right,' said the dog. 'I mean, look at her now. How does she know my favourite colour's blue? Yet there she is, knitting me a blue blanket.'

'She's a great credit to you,' said the hedgehog. 'You must feel very proud.'

'Well, one does one's best.'

When people and animals get old, they need to be cared for. Houses are the same. But as gardens grow old, they become more beautiful each year. The less people interfere with them, the better they become. If a tree falls and someone clears it away, it's gone for ever. If it's left alone, it becomes home to a thousand insects and creeping plants. Fungus grows and the tree slowly melts back into the earth to feed new trees.

When the old lady and the house had been young the garden was already full of ancient trees. Her father had planted more and now they were full grown.

Beneath the trees and bushes, weeds grew thick in tiny jungles. Nettles and dandelions brought butterflies and birds to the garden and behind the secret leaves mice and frogs lived hidden lives. When the old lady's nephew came he cut the lawn but apart from that the garden was left to grow its own way. All around, the other houses had neat tidy rows of flowers, sprayed and weeded in lifeless earth, but here was a complete world where nature lived unharmed.

The lily pond was hidden behind overgrown raspberry canes. The vegetable garden had disappeared under a carpet of grass. When she had been a little girl, the old lady had planted radishes there, in between her father's lettuces. Now even the brick paths had vanished under a coat of moss. Nature wrapped the whole garden in a beautiful blanket and then started on the house.

'That's nice,' said the old lady, when she saw little trees growing in the gutters and ivy creeping across the window-sills.

The dog was very old now and as the summer passed he grew slower and slower. He slept more and more and his dreams of the days when he could jump and play grew faint and quiet. His rubber ball lay behind the armchair collecting dust. The air around him grew still and weary. Nature sighed and waited. The wind slammed the door unheard and the sweet smells of the garden flowed over him unnoticed. In the garden, the animals passed the open doors and saw him lying there far away in his peaceful silence. The mole waited quietly in her tunnel but he no longer took his daily walk. As the first gold leaves of autumn began to fall he climbed into his bed and went to sleep forever.

He was buried beneath the red apple tree that the old lady had planted as a child and when her nephew had smoothed over the sad little mound and put the spade back among the dark cobwebs and broken deck-chairs in the garden shed, they went back to the house and packed her bags.

'It's time for a change,' she said and went to live by the sea. The house stayed behind and went to sleep.

The lawn grew tall and thick and criss-crossed with the tunnels of small animals that had grown up in the shadows and now came out into the open. The creatures that had hidden in the cellars moved up into the empty rooms and as the years passed, the wild garden grew wilder until the house called fourteen lay hidden behind a wall of green.

The Old Dog

He sits by the door
And looks out at the rain
As it falls soft and warm on the lawn.
The summer has nearly faded again
And each winter comes with a little more pain
And a little less fight for the storm.

He sits by the door
Looking right through the rain
At a spot on the far side of space.
He's getting tired of taking the strain,
There are lights going out in the back of his brain,
He's content to withdraw from the race.

Sid the Mosquito

Behind the trees at the end of the lawn, the pond lay hidden by overgrown bushes. The trees hung their branches down to touch the water and at the water's edge tall grass grew full of hidden flowers and butterflies. Birds nesting in the trees flashed across the water catching flies and their voices filled the air with music.

Dragonflies danced in the air like sparkling jewels unseen by anyone except the mice and birds who went to drink at the water's edge. In the pond itself little creatures lived their secret lives. Tiny snails wriggled in the soft mud at the bottom of the pond. Water beetles and worms darted between the roots of water lilies. Beneath the top of the water, mosquito larvae hung like baby caterpillars waiting to become butterflies. Then very early one morning, before the sun was even up, they all changed into mosquitos and flew off into the jungle of soft grass that grew beneath the honeysuckle.

'Can I go and bite something now, Mum?' said a young mosquito called Sid.

'No, dear,' said his mother.

'Oh go on, Mum,' said Sid. 'Everyone knows mosquitos bite things.'

'Not boys,' said his mother. 'Boys don't bite things, only girls do that.' All Sid's sisters giggled and nudged each other and pointed.

'But what am I going to have for my breakfast if I can't bite something?' cried Sid.

'You have to suck pollen out of buttercups, you do,' sneered his eldest sister, and they all giggled again.

'It's not true,' said Sid with tears in his eyes, but it was. His mother tried to explain as gently as she could that boy mosquitos and girl mosquitos were made differently and that with his delicate mouth he just wouldn't be able to bite anything.

'You just go and get your head into a nice dandelion,' she said.

'I'm not sucking soppy flowers,' said Sid. 'Everyone'll laugh at me.'

'No they won't,' said his mother. 'Your father loved pollen. Why, he spent half his life with his head buried in bluebells.'

Sid felt as if someone had played a rotten trick on him. It had been no fun wiggling around in the pond as a larva, dodging out of the way of the horrid dragonflies and the drinking dog and swimming around with his ears full of stagnant water and hedgehog spit. It had been no fun at all and the only thing that had kept him going had been the thought of biting a nice soft human leg. And now they were telling him that all he was going to get was soppy flowers.

'And keep away from the roses until you're grown up,' she added. 'They're much too strong for a young lad like you.'

The sun climbed above the house, sending its clear light through the branches above the pond. The air grew warmer and one by one Sid's sisters all flew off to bite things. While his mother went down to the the shops to bite a greengrocer, Sid kicked his feet in the earth and sulked under a nettle all morning. There was no way he was going to put his head inside a flower and that was final. He was going to bite a human, or at least a dog. He would even settle for a small mouse but certainly not a dandelion.

The morning became the afternoon and Sid grew hungrier and hungrier. As his sisters came and went with tales of blood they had drunk from policemen's necks and sparrows' knees, Sid listened to his tummy rumble until at last he could stand it no longer.

As soon as no one was looking, he flew off to the house next door to bite a baby.

Noises and new smells floated out of the open windows. There were humans inside, laughing and talking and eating. Sid landed on the window-sill and looked at their bare arms. There was a big pink juicy baby sitting on the floor sucking a sock. Sid was about to fly down to it when he noticed one of his three hundred and five sisters sitting on someone's ear. As he watched, a hand flashed through the air and squashed her. Sid turned and fled.

In next-door's garden their dog snored gently under a deck-chair and Sid decided it would be safer to start with him. He landed on the grass, tiptoed across to the sleeping animal, shut his eyes and pounced.

The next thing he knew, he was flying through the air with a sore nose and tears streaming from his eyes.

'Get out of it,' growled an angry voice in the dog's fur.

'Yeah,' said another, 'or we'll pull your wings off.'

'Yeah, that's right,' said a third.

Sid sat up and shook his head. Something dark and horrible leapt out of the dog and landed in front of him. It was an angry flea with a mean look in its eye.

'Listen sonny,' it said, 'that's our dog that is, so watch it. You just push off back to the buttercups where you belong.'

'Yeah, push off,' the third flea said again from somewhere behind the dog's left ear.

Sid crept off into the quiet heart of a big red rose bush and hid behind a sharp thorn. He could hear the fleas all laughing but after a while the dog got up and wandered off and it was peaceful again. His nose was still very sore and he really was very hungry by then so forgetting his mother's advice, he stuck his tongue into the middle of a big red rose.

His mouth was filled with a million wonderful tastes. The pollen tasted like strawberry jam, caramel pudding and black cherry ice cream all rolled into one. As he wriggled his tongue around he picked up the nectar which was even more wonderful, like thick chocolate sauce and creme eggs floating in condensed milk. Of course, Sid was only a little mosquito and had never heard of chocolate or all the other delicious things. All he knew was that what he was eating was totally amazingly completely fantastic and he was feeling sick.

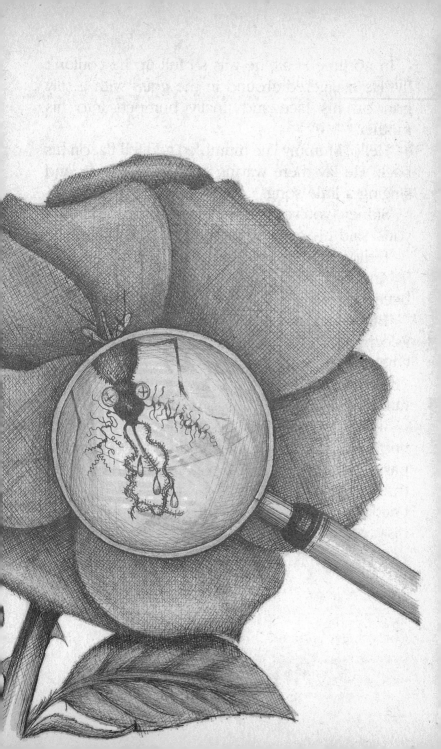

In no time at all, he was so full up he couldn't fly. He staggered around in the grass with a silly grin on his face and finally bumped into his mother.

'Hello, Mummy,' he mumbled and fell flat on his back. He lay there waving his legs in the air and singing a little song.

'Sidney, you've been in the rose bush, haven't you?' said his mother, pretending to be cross.

'Hello, Mummy,' he said again.

'And what's happened to your nose? Have you been fighting?'

'Big flea bashed me,' said Sid and fell fast asleep. Soon he was far away in the land of dreams where huge roses grew as big as flying saucers. The air was filled with raindrops only they weren't raindrops, they were drops of nectar.

Sid dreamt he was floating down a river of nectar in a little boat made of a rose petal. He passed a raft of grass that was sinking fast and the three nasty fleas on board couldn't swim. They cried out for him to save them but he just poked his tongue out at them and sailed by.

On the river banks, children with big soft pink arms begged him to come and bite them as he passed, but he couldn't stop because he was on his way to a special appointment. He dreamt that the Queen of England herself had sent him a telegram requesting his presence at Buckingham Palace where he was to bite her Majesty's left ear, and for pudding he was to have a go at all the royal corgis.

When Sid woke up, it really was raining. His mother had bitten off a piece of grass and covered him with it so only his feet sticking out of the bottom were getting wet. Like all insects every-where he climbed up under a leaf to keep dry and sat next to an old spider, waiting for the rain to pass. The spider kept complaining that when she was a girl it was always nice and sunny and never rained at all.

By the time the sky was clear again, evening was falling and Sid's sisters began to come home. Some flew in alone, some came in twos or threes and other arrived in groups.

Twenty-seven of the sisters hadn't come back yet as they were biting people at a barbecue in next-door's garden. Fourteen had been squashed, twelve had discovered too late what it is that swallows swallow and one had got stuck to some sticky tape on a parcel and was on her way to Australia.

Young lady mosquitos are horrible things. They

bite anything they can get their nasty teeth into. They bite sleeping babies, happy budgerigars and even princesses. And when there's nothing else to bite they bite each other. Sid sat quietly in the corner and listened as the girls sat around telling amazing stories.

'I bit the postman three times,' said one.

'That's nothing,' said one called Sharon. 'I flew right into a bathroom and bit an enormous lady with no clothes on seven times and I tripped over the soap and bruised three of my knees really badly.'

'Well that's nothing at all,' boasted a third sister. 'I flew into an aeroplane, went all the way to America and back and bit twenty-three first class passengers.'

'You're all dead soft, you are,' said the stupidest sister. 'I'm so tough I jumped up and down inside the prickliest thistle in the whole world and bit myself twenty-seven million million times.'

They went on for hours boasting away to each other, each sister trying to be braver and cleverer than the others. Sid listened wide-eyed to their stories. He was an honest little insect and didn't realise they were making them all up. Even when one said she had been to the moon in a space-ship, he believed her.

'And what have you been doing?' they asked Sid. As well as biting everything, young lady mosquitos are very rude to everyone, have dreadful bad breath and lots of spots. Young boy mosquitos on the other hand, because they only eat nectar and pollen, are kind and well behaved and have perfect skin.

'Have you been fighting a ferocious buttercup?' laughed the girls.

'Now just you leave young Sid alone,' said his mother. 'He's had more adventures today than any of you.'

'Ooh, ooh,' sneered the sisters, 'did you get slapped by a daisy?'

'He got hit on the nose by some vicious fleas and doesn't want any trouble from you lot.'

'Fleas, fleas. We hate fleas,' shouted the girls and they all flew off to fight them, except Sharon who stayed behind to rub a dock leaf on her sore knees.

The next morning was perfect. A little cloud of soft mist hung above the pond as the sunshine crept over the trees. Birds stretched their wings and filled the air with a hundred new songs. The dragonflies flashed across the water while butterflies unfolded themselves and flew off across the nettles where busy ladybirds scuttled about. All down the little street the houses were quiet except for the clinking sound of milk bottles.

Sid sat on a twig breathing the damp sweet air. One by one his nasty sisters staggered out from under their leaves. They wandered about swearing a lot. They swore at the birds for being too noisy. They swore at the sunshine for being too bright. They swore at the butterflies for being too beautiful and they swore at the humans for still being in bed when they wanted to bite them. Most of all though, they swore at each other for being mosquitos.

Eventually they all flew off and the pond was peaceful again. Sid flew deep inside an enormous waterlily. It was like being in a great big white tent. He shared his breakfast with a couple of wasps and a family of small brown beetles. One of the wasps was called Arnold and was about the same age as Sid.

Sid tried to tell Arnold about not being able to bite people but the wasp's ears were completely filled up with pollen and he couldn't hear him. Sid tried shouting.

'There's no need to shout,' said Arnold.

'Sorry.'

'What did you say?' said Arnold.

'Nothing,' muttered Sid and flew back to his twig. Nobody seemed to be interested in a little mosquito's problems. It wasn't that he didn't like pollen: it was very nice. And it wasn't that he wanted to be off with his sisters biting people all day long. All he wanted was one little bite, just to prove he could do it. That was all.

He decided to try again and set off towards the house next door. The curtains and windows were all open now. The people were cooking their breakfast and the cat was chasing birds round the edge of the lawn. As Sid sat on the kitchen window-sill, Arnold shot past and dived head first into a jar of marmalade.

Sid flew upstairs and into a bedroom. Inside a small boy was getting dressed. As he leant over to try and do up his shoes, Sid landed on his neck and tried to bite him. He opened his mouth as wide as he could and pushed and shoved and clenched his fists. His ears began to ache and he went bright red in the face but all he could do was dribble.

The little boy went down to the kitchen and Sid sat on the bedside table and cried.

At first there were so many tears in his eyes that he didn't notice the little man standing next to him. Then as his tears grew less he saw him. He

had his back to Sid and didn't seem to have any clothes on. Sid tiptoed over and tried to bite him on the shoulder. To his amazement, his tiny teeth went right into the man and his mouth was filled with sugar.

Sid jumped for joy. Then he noticed the others. There was a whole crowd of them hiding in a box. They didn't seem to notice him at all so he went and bit every one of them. It was like sticking his head in the rose. He felt all happy and giddy. He had done it! He had actually bitten someone.

A bit later on the little boy came back and got the box of jelly babies, but by then Sid was back at the pond telling everyone about his adventure.

Three Sparrows

It was a beautiful hot summer's day and in the cluttered branches of an old apple tree three sparrows were sitting on a twig looking at a baby bird. It was a big fat creature with spiky little wings poking out of its fuzzy baby feathers. It sat hunched up in a tiny nest with a mean look in its eye.

'He's a big boy, your Andrew,' said Gladys, the first sparrow.

'Absolutely enormous,' said Mavis, his proud mother.

'In fact, he's twice as big as you.'

'Lovely, isn't he?' beamed Mavis. 'Who's Mummy's lovely boy, then?'

'He's very big for his size,' said Doris, the third

sparrow.

'Shut up, Doris,' said Gladys. 'He must eat a lot,' she said.

'Eat? Eat? I'll say he eats. Never stops,' said Mavis. 'I don't get a minute's rest.'

'And the other children?' asked Gladys, 'Get on all right with him, do they?'

'Other children?'

'Well, you had five, didn't you?'

'You know, I'd forgotten all about the others,' said Mavis. 'I wonder where they've got to?'

'Probably squashed flat under your precious baby,' muttered Doris.

'What?'

'I said, he's very fat,' said Doris.

'No he's not,' snapped Mavis. 'He's big-boned.'

The young bird opened his beak and let out such a great squawk that the three sparrows fell off the branch. Instinctively Mavis dived into the bushes and came out a few seconds later with a big fat worm.

'I do wish he wouldn't grab his food like that,' said Mavis, pulling her head out of Andrew's gigantic mouth.

'He'll swallow you if you're not careful,' said Gladys.

'He seems a bit simple to me,' said Doris.

'Well you should know,' snapped Gladys.

'He's a lovely boy,' said Mavis, hopping along the twig. 'Who's Mummy's little beauty, then?'

'Cuckoo,' said Andrew.

Ted the Flea

There are some people who think they are better than others because they talk differently or live in an expensive house. Because they've got a bigger car or more money, they look down on everyone else. It's just the same with fleas. Fleas who live on smart dogs think they are superior to fleas that live on cats. Fleas that live on rabbits think they are better than fleas that live on hedgehogs. And fleas that live on humans think they are the greatest fleas in the world.

Ted was the humblest flea of all, for he lived on a rat. It wasn't even a young bright-eyed rat but a wheezing old creature with two yellow teeth and only one ear that lived alone in a rusty tin down a drain.

'You don't know when you're well off,' said Ted's mother. 'There are fleas in China who would give their eye teeth to live in such luxury.'

'No, there aren't,' said Ted.

'I'll no-there-aren't you in a minute, my boy,' snapped his mother.

'Ungrateful, that's what he is,' cursed his granny. 'When I was his age, I er, I er . . .' stuttered the old flea, unable to remember.

'What?' said Ted. 'When you were my age, what?'

'Er, well, when I was your age,' spluttered his granny, 'I was younger.'

'Shut up and drink your blood,' said Ted's mother.

'It's horrible,' said Ted. 'It tastes of dirty washing-up water and mouldy bacon.'

'Ungrateful, that's what he is,' muttered his granny again. 'Children these days don't know when they're well off. When I was his age we had to live on slug dribble and glad we were to get it.'

'Yes, and ant sick,' said Ted's mother.

'Ah, the good old days,' said Ted's granny with a faraway look in her eyes.

'But I'm a vegetarian,' protested Ted.

'Don't be stupid,' snapped his mother.

That night Ted crept off to bed in the rat's scabby ear feeling very sorry for himself. He fell asleep shivering under three greasy hairs in a quilt of green wax and dreamt of a better life. Up above in the outside world it was raining. Thundering water poured down the drain, splashing into the tin as it passed, and the old rat twitched and coughed in its sleep. All night long it rained but asleep in the rat's only ear Ted dreamt of summer fields and the sunshine that he'd never seen. While the rest of his disgusting family snored between the rat's toes, he was far away in a magical land.

The sun was shining brightly in a clear blue sky. It shone down on a field of bright red poppies and gentle grass. In the field, fluffy lambs jumped and played and deep in the wool of the prettiest lamb of all, Ted lay back as a beautiful lady flea fed him on strawberry juice.

'I was offered the chance to live in a queen's armpit,' whispered the beautiful flea in a soft French accent. 'But I turned it down so I could stay with you.'

'Oh,' sighed Ted.

'Oh,' sighed the pretty French flea.

'Oh, you bone idle little scruffbag,' shouted a voice, knocking him out of bed.

Ted sat sniffling on the rat's last remaining whisker and looked out at the wet drain. The rest of his family were having breakfast in the rat's navel but Ted just didn't feel hungry.

'There must be more to life than this,' he thought to himself.

Suddenly, there was a scratching noise from further down the drain and a soaking mouse came scrabbling up the brickwork. Ted saw his chance and as the mouse drew level with the tin, he sprang on to its back and held on tight as the animal climbed out into the garden and the bright spring sunshine.

'Hello,' he called quietly as he explored the mouse's fur. 'Anyone at home?' But there wasn't. He searched from the end of the mouse's tail to the tip of its nose, but there were no other fleas on board. He had the whole creature to himself.

All morning Ted sat on the mouse's head as it bustled around the flower beds eating seeds. There was so much to take in, so many amazing things that he'd never seen before: the grass, the trees and the wonderful sunshine.

For the first time in his life he felt warm and happy. Birds, whose voices he had only heard as distant echoes at the top of the drain, flew in and out of the bushes singing to each other. There were butterflies, red roses, and golden dandelions, and across the lawn a big black cat that came nearer and nearer, tiptoeing towards them without a sound. It shone like polish and its sharp white teeth grew brighter and brighter and larger and larger until they suddenly disappeared into the mouse's fur with a snap that threw Ted high into the air.

Over and over he rolled, until he came crashing down into a world of total darkness in the cat's fur.

'Do you mind?' said a superior voice.

'Really, some people,' said another.

Gradually Ted's eyes grew used to the dark and in front of him he could see the owners of the voices. They were fleas, but quite unlike the fleas he had grown up with. They were fat and shiny, not dull and skinny like Ted's family.

'Hello,' he said, 'I'm Ted.'

'Well, Ted,' said the largest flea, looking down her nose at him. 'You can't stay here.'

'Why not?' asked Ted.

'There isn't any room.'

'But there's lots of room,' said Ted.

'No there isn't,' said the fattest flea. 'You'll have to get off.'

The more Ted protested, the nastier the fleas became. He tried crying but it did no good. They just poked him and tried to make him fall off. In the end he got angry and started calling them all the rude names he'd heard his mother use. They chased him but they were so fat they couldn't catch him. He ran off down the end of the cat's tail where they were far too stuck up to go.

After the cat had eaten the mouse it curled up under a bush and went to sleep. The air was warm and filled with the hum of summer flies. A blackbird hopped about on the lawn digging in the grass. Closer and closer it came until it was right behind the cat. As it bent over to pull a fat worm out of the earth, Ted leapt on to its back and two minutes later he was high in the sky, far above the old house and garden.

As he looked down he saw the cat come out from beneath the bush and jump over the fence into next-door's garden. There were two children playing on the striped lawn and the flower-beds and bushes were all trimmed and cut tidily. There were gardens like that as far as Ted could see. There were people pushing lawnmowers and hanging out washing or just sitting in the sun. In some gardens dogs lay stretched out and a few sparrows and starlings flitted about, but only the garden he had grown up in was wild and full of wonderful overgrown trees. Everywhere else was clean and tidy like a room inside a house. Only his garden was alive with birds and wild animals.

'Mister,' said a tiny red creature tugging at his leg. 'Please, mister, have you come from heaven?'

'Yeah, mister, are you an angel?' said another. The little creatures were bird mites and to them, Ted, who had suddenly appeared from nowhere, was a magical giant.

'I might be,' said Ted, looking down and hanging on for dear life as the bird swooped down into the garden again.

'Cor, can we worship you then, mister?' said the mites, all clamouring round Ted's knees.

'You can give me a present if you like,' said Ted, who was feeling peckish, which was quite funny considering he was sitting on a bird's back.

'We ain't got nuffink, mister,' said the mites.

'What, no food?' asked Ted.

'Only blackbird's blood.'

'Oh well,' sighed Ted. After all he was a flea and although he had told his mother that he was a vegetarian, he knew that fleas live on blood.

The blackbird landed in a tree and as Ted curled up for a quiet afternoon sleep, it began singing at the top of its voice. Ted tried covering his ears with all six legs but it did no good. Another blackbird flew down and the two of them sang even louder. For the first time since he'd left the old rat, Ted wondered if it had been such a good idea.

'There must be somewhere I can go,' he thought to himself, 'somewhere I won't get jumped on or chased or deafened.'

Round the side of the house behind a great tangle of bushes there was a hole in the fence. Sometimes when the dog next door got fed up with her neat and tidy world where everything smelt of washing-up liquid and plastic, she would squeeze through the fence and come into the old garden.

Ted watched as she ambled around the edge of the flower-beds sniffing every leaf as if it was a beautiful flower. In the dog's own garden the grass was so short that the lawn was no more than earth painted green. In Ted's garden, since the old lady had gone, the grass had grown rich and soft. It reached up to the dog's knees and she rolled over and over in it as if she were swimming through treacle.

Ted looked down. The dog was right underneath him on her back. Tiny black specks flashed in her brown fur, black flecks that looked like other fleas. Ted crawled to the tip of the blackbird's tail and jumped.

'Get out of it,' growled an angry voice in the dog's fur.

'Yeah,' said another, 'or we'll pull your wings off.'

'Yeah, that's right,' said a third.

'I haven't got any wings,' Ted shouted. Something dark leapt out of the dog and landed in front of him. It was an angry flea with a mean look in its eye.

'It's all right lads,' he called. 'He's one of us.'

'We thought you was a mosquito,' said another flea, coming out of the fur.

'Yeah, we've had a lot of trouble with mosquitos,' said the first flea. 'Coming here and trying to eat our dog.'

Ted told the two fleas, Dick and Rick, about the old rat in the drain and how he'd run away to find a better life. He told them about the mouse and the cat fleas and the red mites.

'They're rubbish, cat fleas,' said Dick.

'Not as rubbish as hedgehog fleas,' said Rick.

'Yes they are,' said Dick.

'Not.'

'You want a fight?'

'Yeah,' said Rick and the two fleas jumped on

each other but before either of them could hit the other, the air was filled with a loud whining noise and a huge cloud of mosquitos came crashing down on them.

Fleas appeared from all parts of the dog, which was sitting by the house scratching itself. Its fur was full of struggling mosquitos all tangled up and swearing at the tops of their voices. The dog fleas charged into them with their legs flying.

'Maybe I should've stayed on the blackbird,' thought Ted, 'or even on the old rat.' As the battle went on all around him, he crept off to a quiet corner feeling quite homesick. Was there nowhere he could go to be happy?

The dog gave one great scratch and Ted went sailing through the air. Over and over he tumbled until he vanished into a world of total darkness. As he fell further away from the sunlight, sweet familiar awful smells drifted up towards him. He was back in his drain, and the stagnant water and the rat's bad breath that had once made him feel so ill now smelt warm and friendly. He looked down and far below the weak light shone on the lid of the rat's tin. As he raced by he reached out and grabbed its only whisker. He crawled into the rat's ear and lay there exhausted.

'You bone idle little scruffbag,' shouted a voice, knocking him out of bed.

'Hello, Mum,' said Ted. 'I've just had an awful dream.'

'I'll awful-dream you in a minute, my boy,' snapped his mother. His ears were aching and his head was ringing but Ted was smiling. He really was home again. And no matter how bad things sometimes seemed, he knew that it was where he wanted to stay forever.

The Rabbits

Right at the bottom of the garden behind the rusty car was where the rabbits lived. Their burrows peered out like black eyes between the twisted roots of trees that grew out of a bank of earth beneath the tall fence. Honeysuckle grew up from the roots, almost covering the fence and reaching its winding arms up into the branches. On the other side of the fence, past a thick forest of nettles and brambles, was a tow path that ran behind all the houses as it followed a canal into the middle of the town.

The almost endless honeycomb of tunnels that the rabbits lived in spread out from the fence like a huge underground city. It reached up the garden right to the brick walls of the cellars below the house. Through tiny cracks in the cement the rabbits could peer into the cellars and see the rats scurrying about through the old boxes and coal. In the other direction the warren went out under the canal, up on to the far bank where there was a field of wasteland covered in broken concrete and rubbish.

In the tunnels lived a rambling wild family of rabbits. They were not the shy secretive animals of children's stories who only come out at night to nibble the lettuces. These were loud fearless rabbits who jumped on the lettuces and ate the roses, rabbits who shouted and swore and sang rude songs and laughed and spat and threw stones into the pond.

On beautiful summer days when the garden was half asleep in the warm sunshine and the birds were singing softly in the wild strawberries and the whole world seemed to be standing still, they would go crashing through the grass, jumping on everyone's dreams. From their broken-down tunnels they spread noise and chaos to every corner of the garden. They went through the hedge, attacked next-door's cat and bit the heads off the flowers.

'Go away,' mumbled the hedgehogs as they dozed under the geraniums.

'Rock and roll,' shouted the rabbits and they crashed through the undergrowth, snapping twigs and kicking up the molehills.

'Go away,' called Elsie the mole from her tunnel.

''Ere we go, 'ere we go, 'ere we go,' sang the rabbits as they ran laughing in a line round the lawn.

All afternoon, all evening and most of the night the racket would go on. There were rabbits creating chaos everywhere. When it was dark they tunnelled into other gardens and chewed all the heads off the marigolds and at midnight when the humans had just got into their beds and turned out the lights, they knocked the lids off the dustbins.

Only in the early mornings when the rabbits were sleeping was it peaceful in the garden. The sun came up, a big fuzzy circle in the mist that hung over the canal. Birds woke up, stretched their wings and slipped away through the trees. A hedgehog shuffled across the lawn making dark tracks in the white frost as it hurried back to its bed. From the rabbit warren came a chorus of loud snores punctuated with coughs and sneezes. From each tunnel little clouds of grey steam drifted across the garden carrying the smell of damp fur and mouldy grass.

As morning reached lunchtime sleepy rabbits would begin to emerge yawning into the daylight. They staggered through the bushes snorting and spitting and tripping over the dock leaves. By early afternoon they were banging and crashing away again as loud as the day before. At least once a week one of them fell into the pond and splashed around cursing until it managed to scramble out again.

'I've had enough of this,' said an old crow. 'I don't
know what's got into them, but it's got to stop.'

'What can we do?' said Elsie the mole. 'If you
say anything they just ignore you.'

'They weren't always like this,' said Ethel the old
chicken. 'When I was young rabbits were sweet
and fluffy. Now they're like wild animals.'

'They are wild animals,' said a rat. 'We all are.'

'I'm not,' said Ethel proudly. 'I'm domesticated.'

'Well, we've got to do something,' said the old
crow.

The next morning while the rabbits lay asleep in their wildest dreams, the hedgehogs and the crows rolled big stones into the entrances of the burrows. One by one they blocked them up until only the main tunnel was left open.

Then all the animals in the garden sat in a big semi-circle round the warren entrance and watched for the rabbits to come out. They slept late that day but the animals sat patiently waiting. Animals are not like humans, they don't get bored so quickly. Moles and slugs don't get bored at all.

At last the rabbits began to stir. From inside the blocked tunnels came the sounds of swearing and a lot of scrabbling commotion. At last some of them found the open entrance and came blundering out.

'Who's been blocking up our tunnels?' they shouted.

'We have,' said a huge crow, towering over the sleepy rabbits, the sun flashing on his large bill.

'Oh yeah,' said Ernie the rabbit, nervously. 'Well you got no right.'

'Yeah,' said his mate Dave.

'We're fed up with all your noise,' said the crow.

'Oh yeah?' said Ernie.

'Yes,' said the crow, leaning right over the rabbit until his bill was touching its fur.

'Why do you have to rush round making such a racket all the time?' asked the hedgehogs.

'Why can't you let us live in peace?' said the old

chicken.

'Go and look in the other gardens,' said a blackbird. 'There's nothing there for us. You can see that and you can see that it's like that for miles and miles. Our garden is a special place, a place where no one comes to kill the weeds or the insects or to cut down the trees. It's a place where we can live together in peace, yet you insist on spoiling it all. Why can't you live quietly like the rest of us?'

Arthur, the oldest rabbit, came to the front and said, 'I'll tell you why.'

Arthur was the oldest animal in the garden. He was so old that none of the other animals could remember a time when he hadn't been there.

'I'll tell you why we shout and laugh and sing,' he said, and he told them the terrible story of what had happened.

'It's all right for you,' he said. 'Most of you never leave this garden from the day you are born until the day you die. Oh, yes, some of you birds fly up in the sky but from up there everything looks small and safe like a child's toy. But us rabbits go out into the world and come into contact with man. We have seen the awful things he can do and

we have learned to fear him.'

All the animals felt a sudden cold wind run through their hearts. They had never heard talk like that before. They all stared at the ground so no one else would see the fright in their eyes.

'Across the canal,' the old rabbit continued, 'across the wasteland, over the road hidden behind tall trees, there is an evil place. Two years ago some of us went there and we saw such terrifying things that we knew we could never be sweet and fluffy again.'

The sun was at its highest point in the blue summer sky. A haze of heat shimmered in the air yet all the animals were shivering. None of them knew what the rabbits had seen but they could tell it had been something almost too awful to talk about.

'Behind the evil place,' said Arthur, 'We found a row of dustbins and when, as animals do, we climbed into them to find food, we looked into the face of death. When we pushed off the lids the air was filled with the sweet smell of roses like a summer's day. But it was the middle of winter and there were no flowers there, just two blind rabbits with their eyes and bodies full of ladies' perfume. They were still alive so we led them back across the river to the safety of the garden. And that is why we shout and swear and dance and sing, for all the other animals that are still in those awful places.'

The animals stood silent with an aching pain in their hearts. The young ones felt frightened and clung to their parents who were filled with a terrible anger.

'Isn't there anything we can do?' said the crow.

'No, nothing,' said Arthur.

'There must be something,' said a sparrow, but he knew there wasn't. They all knew there was nothing any animal could do. They knew that every single animal in the world survived only because man let them.

'That's why we shout and laugh,' said Arthur.
'We could all be dead tomorrow.'

'Couldn't you shout and laugh quietly?' said Ethel. She was an old hen and didn't really understand. The only human she had ever known had been the old lady who'd lived in the house and she'd always been really kind.

'We could eat the electric cables,' said the rats. 'That'd teach them.'

'You do that already,' said the crow. 'We could build nests and block up their chimneys.'

'You do that already,' said the rats.

'Maybe if we all kept out of their way, they'd leave us alone,' said the old chicken.

'If only we could talk to them,' said a hedgehog.

'It wouldn't make any difference,' said Arthur. 'The only thing that will make men change is other men.' And he was right. Only the children growing up today can make tomorrow different.

Bob the Slug

Behind the apple trees, past the overgrown pond, was the old vegetable garden. Once the earth had been neat and filled with rows of vegetables and fruit, but now nobody went there any more and the ground belonged to nature again.

Under an old brown cabbage that no one had wanted, hidden in a twilight world of soft green slime, lived Bob the slug. He was fat and black and sticky and shone like a piece of polished coal.

Every morning Bob and his family slithered out from their damp home and began to eat. They ate every green thing that lay in their path and each day they had to slither a little bit further to find something new.

'One day,' said Bob, swallowing a daisy, 'We'll

have eaten the whole world and there'll be nothing left to eat.'

'That's rubbish,' said his uncle Quentin.

'No, this is rubbish,' said Bob, biting into a mouldy plum.

'And you are dinner,' said Barry the hedgehog, eating them both and saving the world.

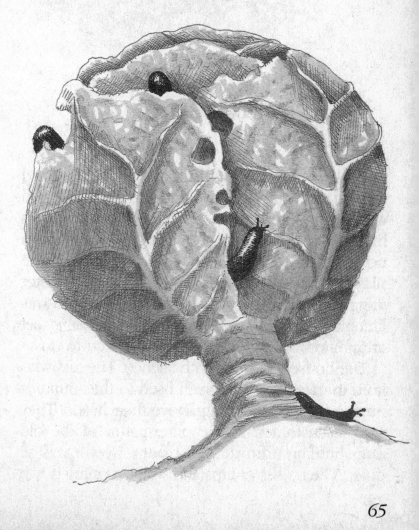

The Rats

After the old lady moved away dampness spread through the empty house and the air grew tired waiting for someone to breathe it. The dampness brought cold, so even on a sunny day the house never grew warm. Behind the wallpaper the plaster began to crumble and behind the plaster tiny plants began to grow in the moisture that was creeping up the walls. And in the larder, sweet crumbs of food grew mould and turned to dust.

The house was filled with silence. The rats who lived in the cellars had been used to the sound of human footsteps moving above their heads. They were accustomed to the pitter-patter of the old dog shuffling from room to room. Now it was all quiet. The noises of taps and water running down pipes and drains, the muffled sound of the radio, had all stopped. Now there was absolutely nothing.

At first the rats hadn't noticed. The noises had been like the sound of cars out in the street that are there all the time so you aren't aware of them. They all felt uneasy but no one knew why. Then one day a young rat called Derek stopped chewing the electric cable and looked up at the silent ceiling.

'Listen,' he said.

'What?' said another rat. 'I can't hear anything.'

'Exactly,' said Derek.

Everyone stopped what they were doing and listened. The house was completely silent. Even the ticking of the kitchen clock had stopped.

'She's probably taken the dog for a walk,' said Derek's mum.

'But there's always some sort of noise,' said Derek.

'Nn nttthhhnnk mmms nggn mmmggyy,' said a voice from the shadows.

'For goodness sake, Neville,' snapped Derek's mum. 'How many times have I told you not to talk with your mouth full?'

'Nnnnggyy, nnnmm.'

'NEVILLE!!!'

'Sorry, Mum.'

'Come here, and bring that sock.'

'What sock?'

'Neville, don't try and pull the wool over my eyes.'

'He's too busy pulling it over his own eyes,' sniggered Derek.

'I haven't got a sock,' said Neville.

'Well, what were you chewing then?' said their mum.

'Er, umm, a sausage,' lied Neville.

'Show me.'

'Er, I've eaten it all.'

'Well in that case,' said his mother, 'you won't want any supper, will you?'

Neville started crying. In the dark corner his small shadowy shape could be seen shaking as his tears fell on to the floor. The sun came in through the cellar window and landed on his little wet feet. His mother went over and put her arms round him.

'It's all right,' she said, tickling his ears.

'I do try Mum, honest,' he sobbed. 'I just can't stop myself.'

'But where do you keep getting them from? Socks don't grow on trees.'

Neville went silent and hung his head. He shuffled his feet and clung to his mother with his eyes tight shut.

'Well?'

'Squirrels,' said Neville, hiding in his mother's apron. He told her that when the squirrels next door ran along the clothes-line to get to the bird table, some of the washing fell on to the lawn.

'Are there any knickers?' whispered Neville's brother, Trevor.

'TREVOR, I HEARD THAT!!'

'Sorry, Mum.'

'And stop sniggering, you lot,' said the mother rat.

'Sorry, Mum,' they all chorused.

Up in the house, the larder was empty apart from some ancient jars of bottled fruit on the top shelf. It had been ages since any of them had had a really good meal. They could hardly remember when they had last chewed up a lump of lard or some chocolate. It had been autumn when the old lady had gone and there had still been plenty to eat out in the garden. It was winter now and food was beginning to get scarce.

Derek peered cautiously round the larder door. The kitchen was deserted and smelt damp. He sniffed the air for clues but there was nothing, just the stale emptiness. In the old days there had been a warmth in the air, a soft mixture of sponge cakes and old lady's perfume and toffees, but now it was all gone.

The other rats followed him nervously as he ran across the kitchen and out into the dark hall. Most of them had never been up into the house before and they felt frightened. Everywhere was so big. They were in a land of giants where the ceilings seemed as far away as the sky.

A thin layer of dust had settled on everything like dirty frost and the house was as silent as the middle of the night. Even the wheel in the electricity meter had stopped moving. Behind the front door was a tumbled pile of letters and newspapers.

'We'll eat those later,' said Derek as he led them up the stairs. Neville, who was little more than a baby, bounced up and down by the bottom step.

'I can't get up,' he cried.

'Well, go back down to the cellar,' said Derek.

'I'm frightened,' cried Neville.

'It's all right,' said Derek. 'Mum and Dad are down there.'

'Take me,' wailed Neville.

'Why?'

'I'm frightened of the light,' cried the baby rat.

Derek climbed down and led him through the bright kitchen into the larder. By the familiar hole that led down to the cellar, Neville clutched his big brother's fur and whispered: 'I wasn't really frightened.'

'I know you weren't,' smiled Derek.

'If there are any socks up there,' said Neville,

feeling brave again, 'you'll save me one, won't you?'

'Of course,' said Derek. The baby rat ran down the tunnel into the cellar while Derek went back and led the others upstairs. Without him to lead them they had felt nervous and hadn't moved until he'd got back.

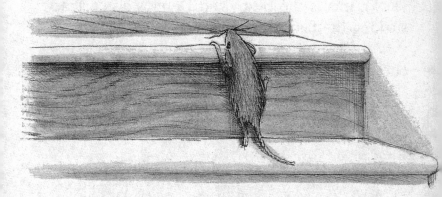

'It doesn't look as if there's much to eat up here,' said Derek, as they went from room to room. All the furniture was still there but the old lady had taken everything else. The cupboards were bare and so were all the drawers apart from hairpins and talcum powder. They chewed their way into the mattresses but there was nothing there. They chewed their way into the armchairs but all they found was one boiled sweet covered in hairs. It was the same in every room, a squashed toffee here and a soggy crisp there, but nothing else. It wasn't until they got to the bathroom that they found any real food.

'It must be another larder,' said Derek. 'The old lady must have kept food up here in case she got hungry in the middle of the night.'

'Oh, wow, this is fantastic,' said Trevor as he nibbled all the bristles off the lavatory brush.

'I bet it's not as good as this,' said Derek, licking a hole right through the middle of the soap.

'No, this is the best,' said Derek's sister Tracy, sucking the flannel.

'You haven't tried this yet,' said someone else, chewing the lino round the toilet.

There were so many wonderful things to eat, it was difficult to know where to start. There were half-used tubes of toothpaste that tasted like strawberries and roll-on deodorants that tasted like old armpits. Down the side of the bath there were bars of soap covered with delicious fluff and when Derek ate a hole in a laundry basket he found a sock for his baby brother. It was better than the socks Neville got from next door because it was very old and hadn't been in the washing machine. The old lady's bathroom was like a fancy restaurant with exotic meals from all over the world.

Over the next few months, the rats stripped the house. Even the oldest rat, Uncle Trubshaw, who had eaten nothing but oven scrapings all his life, was persuaded to come up from the cellar, and ate three hot-water bottles. Young Neville, with a bit of pushing and shoving, managed to get upstairs where he vanished into the laundry basket. When he came out a fortnight later he was incredibly fat and smelt very strange.

But all good things come to an end and after a few months there was nothing left but some unpleasant strips of green elastic and a shrivelled brown thing covered in hairy mould. Neville ate the elastic but nobody would touch the hairy thing.

'I'm sure I saw it move,' said Uncle Trubshaw and after that no one, not even Trevor, who had eaten the underneath of the toilet seat and one of those things you put in the water to make it go blue, would go near it.

They searched in the darkest corners, eating more and more indigestible things until there was nothing left they could get their teeth into. They ate the letters on the front doormat and then they ate the doormat. Neville tried to eat the telephone but cut his tongue on the '3' button. In the dining room there was wallpaper covered in strawberries but it tasted like two-hundred-year-old mildew. They cleared the tiniest crumbs from the kitchen and licked every last drop of spilt gravy until the whole room sparkled and looked cleaner than it had done for fifty years.

It was quite a long time since the old lady had left and the dampness that had begun in the cellar had now reached the roof. Any warmth that the sun put in through the windows was soaked up straight away and everywhere felt cold and clammy. Down in the cellar the rats huddled together in their nests and began to grow thin.

'Winter will be here again soon,' said Derek's mother. 'We should be warm and fat and ready for the snow, not feeling cold and hungry.'

They had spent so long inside the house that by the time they went back to the garden all the summer's fruits and berries had been taken by the other animals. To make matters worse, next-door's cat had discovered their tunnel out of the cellar and spent hours waiting in front of it. It was only safe to go out late at night when the cat was indoors.

'Are we all here?' said Uncle Trubshaw.

'I think so,' said Derek. 'There should be twenty-three of us.'

'Twenty-two,' said his mother, coming in from the garden. 'I'm afraid next-door's cat just got Trevor as he was trying to climb up the clothes line.'

'Oh, not Trevor,' wailed Neville.

'There, there,' said his mother. 'It's one of those things. It happens to us rats all the time.'

'It's not that,' snivelled Neville.

'Well, what is it then?' said his mother, stroking his ears.

'I lent him three caterpillars last week and he hasn't paid me back yet,' said Neville.

Over the next couple of weeks things went from bad to worse. Humans came to the house, stomping round the bare floors in big shoes. Down in the cellar the rats crept in behind a loose brick and hid until the thunder above their heads moved away. The humans left but the rats were too frightened to go back upstairs except in the middle of the night. Besides, there was nothing up there for them now.

All they had to eat were a few soggy cardboard boxes and a packet of firelighters. Soon they were reduced to grubbing round in the garden for the other animals' leftovers. As the weather got colder and colder the rats got thinner and thinner. Next-door's cat got Derek's dad and then three of his cousins. No matter how careful they were, the cat seemed to be one step ahead of them. As autumn turned to winter, the cat stayed indoors by the fire but by then there were only six rats left.

'It looks like you're the head of the family now, young Derek,' said Uncle Trubshaw.

'But you're the oldest, Uncle,' said Neville. 'It should be you.'

'Nay lad, I'm too old for all that,' said Uncle Trubshaw. He wasn't too old at all, he was too crafty. He knew that whoever was head of the family would have to sort out the problem of the cat and find them some food.

'Has anyone got any ideas?' said Derek.

'Me, me!' shouted Neville, jumping up and down.

'Well?' said the others.

'Why don't we go out into the street and–' he began, but Uncle Trubshaw went pale and shook his head.

'Out of the garden, you mean?' he said.

'Yes,' said Neville.

'Nay lad,' said Uncle Trubshaw, 'I've never been out of this garden all my life and I'm not going to start now.'

'Have you got a better idea then?' said Derek.

'Aye lad,' said the old rat, 'I have.'

'What?'

'We have to kill the cat.'

'Kill the cat?' said Derek. 'You must be mad. How on earth are we going to do that?'

'Aye lad, we have to kill the cat,' continued Uncle Trubshaw, ignoring Derek's question. 'And when we've killed it, we can eat it.'

'Oh, that's revolting,' said Neville, sucking the insides out of a woodlouse.

'It's ridiculous,' said Derek, and the others agreed.

'Neville's right,' said Derek's mother. 'We have to leave here. While you were all out today there were more humans in the house.'

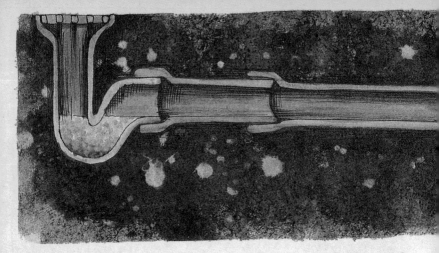

The next day Derek squeezed through the metal grating in the cellar floor and wriggled through the narrow pipe until he was in the drain under the street. The drain ran down the middle of the street and into an enormous tunnel as tall as a man. Derek could tell it was as tall as a man because just as he was about to jump down into it, a man went by carrying a torch.

There was a lot of wonderful food floating down the middle of the tunnel but Derek ignored it and followed the man towards the centre of town. From the distance a thousand new and exciting smells rushed towards him. Other rats looked out of side drains as he passed. Some smiled and waved but most just looked and then disappeared.

'Psst,' said a voice as he passed. Derek ignored it and carried on after the man.

'Oi, Derek,' called the voice. Derek spun round and there was his little brother Trevor.

'Trevor!' he cried and ran over to him. Trevor
was fat and bright-eyed and made Derek look
even thinner and scruffier than he was.

'Mum said the cat got you,' said Derek.

'It did, but I dribbled on its tongue and it spat
me out,' said Trevor. He led Derek down the
narrow drains until they came to a round brick
chamber. There were other rats there and they
were all sleek and well fed.

'See that pipe,' said Trevor, pointing towards
the top of the chamber. 'That leads up to the best
Italian restaurant in the world and out the back are
the best dustbins in the world.'

'There's enough for all of us,' said one of the
other rats.

'Yes, no more toilet seats for me,' laughed
Trevor.

Derek went back to the old house to fetch the remains of his family. That night they went round the garden and said goodbye to all their friends and the following morning they left the old house forever. Even Uncle Trubshaw went with them. He moaned and complained and shook like a leaf but, although he was frightened of the outside world, he was even more frightened of being left alone.

'I'm only coming to make sure you get there safely,' he said. 'I'm not staying.'

He said it every day for the rest of the winter, but by the spring when he was fatter and fitter than he'd been for years, he made sure he only said it when there was no one to hear it.

Delilah the Spider

Delilah the spider sat very still in the corner of the window and waited. There was a fat bluebottle buzzing round the empty room and she knew if she waited long enough it would get caught in her web. A window is the best place for a spider's web because flies spend half their lives crashing into the glass. If they are outside they keep trying to get in, and if they are inside they keep trying to get out.

'Insects are very stupid,' thought Delilah, 'but very tasty.'

A couple of mosquitos that she was saving for lunch wriggled in their silk prison and a blue-tit hung on the window trying to peck them through the glass.

'Birds are very stupid, too,' thought Delilah, 'but I wouldn't want to eat one.'

It was a beautiful clear autumn morning and when the sun had warmed the air Delilah had gone outside and laid three hundred and twenty eggs. They were wrapped in a soft yellow cocoon under the window-sill, sheltered from the wind and rain. Next summer they would hatch and her babies would eat their way down the honeysuckle into the garden. Some of them would wriggle through the gap into the house and Delilah would probably eat them.

'Babies are very stupid,' she thought, 'but very tender.'

When she had finished laying her eggs she had come back into the house and eaten her husband, Nigel.

'Husbands are very stupid,' she thought, 'and very slow.'

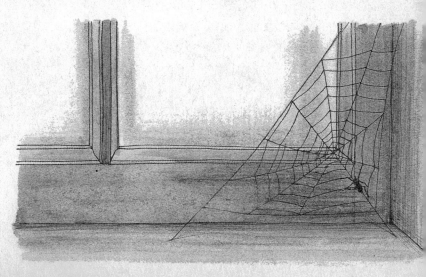

The bluebottle flew round and round the bare light bulb and then dived straight into Delilah's web. It hung there caught by its leg and buzzed furiously. The louder it buzzed and wriggled the more it got caught and the more it got caught the louder it buzzed.

'Look, stupid fly, do you think you could keep the noise down?' snapped Delilah. 'I've got a terrible headache.'

She raced across the silken ladders and rolled the fly up into a parcel, but even when she had wrapped it tight it kept buzzing, so she ate it.

'The mosquitos will keep till tomorrow,' she thought.

There were other spiders in the room, but none on Delilah's window. She had chased them away into the dark corners where all they ever caught were dust mites and midges.

'Spiders are stupid,' said Delilah.

'You think everyone's stupid, don't you?' said a little brown spider called Norma from behind the skirting board.

'That's the only intelligent thing you've ever said,' replied Delilah.

'I think you're horrible,' said the little brown

spider.

'Two intelligent remarks in one day,' sneered Delilah. 'If you're not careful your pathetic little brain will explode.'

Norma said nothing, not because her brain had exploded, but because she was busy thinking of a way to get rid of Delilah.

It was bad enough now the house was empty, without Delilah making everyone's life a misery. There was no one to open the windows so hardly any flies came in. Without humans there were no smells of sticky jam and pies to attract them. What few bits of food the old lady had left had been eaten by the rats. It was all right for the spiders out in the garden, but as everyone knows there are thousands of spiders to every square yard and they certainly wouldn't make room for all the house spiders.

'It's not as if she's anything special like a tarantula,' said Norma. 'She's just a common house spider like the rest of us.'

'She's got the best place in the room and won't let any of us near it,' said Norma's neighbour Sybil.

'You don't have to tell me,' agreed Norma. 'Look what happened when Edwina tried to make a web at the other end of the window.'

'Well yes, I know,' said Sybil. 'She got eaten. I mean, Delilah even ate her own husband.'

'Something will have to be done,' said Norma with a firm stamp of several feet.

Something had to be done. That was obvious. The rest of the spiders, from the coal black shadows of the cellar to the draughty slates on the roof, all managed to live together with no trouble. Sometimes if a strange spider came too close to another's web it got eaten but that was perfectly natural and no one got upset about it. The spider doing the eating had a friendly word with its dinner and everyone knew where they were.

Delilah on the other hand had been nothing but trouble since the day she'd hatched. Within a week she had eaten all her brothers and sisters and her mother. She was as rude and vicious as she could be to everyone. If she couldn't eat them she swore at them. Something had to be done.

'Maybe we could set fire to her web while she's asleep,' suggested Sybil.

'Only humans can do that,' said Norma.

'Maybe we could get a wasp to sting her,' said Sybil.

'Do you want to go and ask one?' asked Norma. Sybil didn't. She knew that wasps were one of the spiders' greatest enemies.

'Well, we've got to do something,' she said.

'It's all right,' said Norma. 'I have a plan.'

Norma's plan was the sort of plan that you make up as you go along. She knew what she wanted to do but she wasn't quite sure how to do it.

Every night under cover of darkness, all the spiders from the upstairs rooms built a huge web across the other side of the room from Delilah. Delilah could see it growing each day but she was far too important to take any interest in it. She was more concerned with her dinner. Since she had eaten the two mosquitos three days before she hadn't caught a single thing and was beginning to feel hungry. She slid down to the floor and stole a flea from Sybil's web and when Sybil protested she ate her.

'Not only are spiders stupid,' she said, 'they taste rotten.' The other spiders said nothing. Across the room they hid under their gigantic web and waited.

In the next room there was a broken window that had been covered up with cardboard. The spiders chewed at the sticky tape until the cardboard fell away. A blast of cold air blew into the room and ten minutes later two huge flies came through the hole and flew straight into the trap the spiders had woven behind it. That night the spiders carried the two flies up into the giant web and wrapped them up just enough to stop them escaping but not to stop them buzzing loudly.

Across the room Delilah woke up and heard the imprisoned flies. She could see them right in the middle of the web the stupid spiders had made and her mouth started watering. She scuttled round the wall and out along the silk rope towards the delicious feast. She was so hungry she felt quite dizzy and didn't notice the other spiders hiding at the corners of the web with their teeth in the threads. She reached the flies and as she did so the whole web went crashing to the ground.

'Stupid spiders,' thought Delilah as she ate the flies. 'Can't even build a web properly.'

'Delilah, Delilah,' called a voice softly from above.

'Drop dead,' snarled Delilah.

'Are you enjoying your last meal?' called the voice.

'Last meal?' laughed Delilah. 'I'll eat you next, idiot.'

'I don't think so,' said the voice.

Delilah looked round. Through the tangle of the web she could see the white walls of the room. There was something strange about them, though. They had become all shiny like glass. Suddenly, she realised where she was but by then it was too late. Round and round she ran but it was no use.

'Bye-bye, Delilah,' called the voice. It was Norma, sitting on the bath tap, looking down into Delilah's prison.

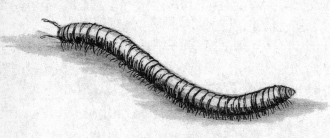

George the Millipede

George the millipede had a terrible pain in one of his feet. It had been hurting him ever since he had tripped over a broken bottle in the front garden. For days he had slithered around with a peculiar wiggle. The other insects looked the other way when he went by so he wouldn't see them smiling.

'The trouble is,' he complained to anyone who would listen, 'I can't tell which foot it is.' With two hundred and forty feet to choose from it was hardly surprising. When you have toothache it doesn't always hurt in the right place. George's foot was the same. One minute he thought it was foot eighty-six on the left and the next it seemed to be foot one hundred and thirty-two on the right. Sometimes it was just behind his head and at others right down the far end.

'I know,' said his brother, Lionel. 'If I kick all your legs really hard, when I kick the sore one it will hurt more than the others and then we'll know which one it is.'

Millipedes are not very bright. They are even more stupid than sheep, so George thought it seemed like a good idea.

By the time Lionel had kicked a hundred of his legs, George was beginning to wonder if it had been such a good idea after all. His eyes were watering and every part of him felt sore. Lionel was so exhausted he could hardly stand and was weaving about the lawn like a drunk worm.

'We can't give up now,' he said and stupid George agreed.

'Ow, ouch, ow, ouch,' he cried as Lionel worked his way down his side. And then at last he cried: 'OWWW!!'

'That's it,' cried Lionel. 'That's the one.' He ran off to get a piece of dock leaf, but when he got back he had lost his place and had to kick George another twenty times until he found it again.

'Ohh, that feels good,' sighed George as he wriggled his bad foot into the dock leaf and limped home.

'Why didn't you just rub all your feet into the leaf?' said George's mother, who wasn't as stupid as her two sons. 'That would've cured it.'

George went bright red and spun round to catch his brother, but Lionel had slipped away across the dandelions.

Autumn

Between gold leaves
The butterfly
Folds its wings,
Soon to die.

Plants shrink back
Into the ground
As winter comes
Without a sound.

The days grow dark,
The air grows cold,
Nature sleeps
And time grows old.

Barry the Hedgehog

Across the lawn behind the old apple trees stood a wooden shed full of lawnmowers and broken deck-chairs. Inside the shed there were cobwebs and dust and the air smelt of oily rags and dried grass. There was a wooden floor that groaned and creaked when anyone walked on it, and under the floor, snuggled into the warm dry earth, lived a family of hedgehogs.

For as long as anyone could remember they had lived there, sheltered from the wind and rain in soft dark nests of grass and newspapers.

Every spring, as the days grew brighter and warmer, they woke from their long sleep. They yawned and stretched and staggered out into the twilight to spend the summer out in the garden.

But now it was winter and time to rest. The leaves had fallen in golden piles and the shady corners where the hedgehogs had lived all summer were now open to the sky. Their hearts began to beat more slowly and their eyelids grew heavy. All round the garden they stopped what they were doing and lifted their faces to the chilly air. One by one they made their way back to the warm nest below the shed, where they curled up and fell into a deep sleep full of dreams of sunshine and soft slugs.

'Come on, Barry,' said a mother hedgehog to her young son. 'Time for bed.'

'Shan't,' said Barry.

'Come on now, there's a good boy.' But he just ignored her.

Barry had been nothing but trouble since the day he'd been born. His brothers and sisters had always behaved like hedgehogs should. They snuffled noisily round the garden eating slugs and earwigs and knocking milk bottles over. Barry kept squeezing through the hedge and stealing next-door's cat food. And while everyone else slept the afternoons away under the rhubarb Barry rolled around collecting squashed plums on his prickles.

'I'm not tired,' he said.

'Don't be silly,' said his mother. 'It's half-past October. You must be tired.'

'Well I'm not,' said Barry, jumping in a puddle. 'Anyway, I think hibernating's really silly.'

Barry's mother decided to leave him to it. When Barry got obstinate the best thing to do was to ignore him. She crawled under the shed and nuzzled into the nest. The air was filled with the smell of damp hedgehogs and a chorus of gentle snoring.

'I'll fetch him later,' she thought to herself, but in no time at all she was fast asleep.

'I'm staying awake, me,' said Barry to a sparrow, 'all winter.'

'Idiot,' said the sparrow and flew off.

Round the back of the shed was an overgrown pile of rubbish. At the bottom of the pile under brambles and old prams was a rusty kettle and it was there that Barry decided to live.

'I'm not going back under the shed with them,' he said, 'not ever.'

He collected some leaves and grass and pushed them into the kettle. He chewed up the fat worms that had been hiding under the leaves and climbed into his new home.

'This is great,' he said to himself, 'better than that rotten shed.'

A crowd of starlings was gathering in the trees. Hundreds of them sat in long lines on the branches and across the roof of the house getting ready to go on holiday. The air was muddled up with their endless chattering.

'Oi,' shouted Barry, sticking his head out of his new home, 'come and see my house.'

'It's just an old kettle,' laughed the starlings.

'I'm staying awake all winter, me,' he shouted.

'Idiot,' chorused two thousand three hundred and forty-seven starlings and flew off to warm African gardens.

'Come back here and say that,' shouted Barry when they were out of sight.

The next few weeks were great. With all his family asleep, there was no one to tell him what to do. There was no one to tell him when to get up, no one to tell him when to sleep and no one to tell him to be quiet. He rolled on his back in the mud, spat in the pond and shouted swear words he'd heard the rabbits use.

Fat and wicked, he sat in the little clearing in front of his house surrounded by young squirrels.

'Say another one,' squeaked the squirrels.

'BOTTOMS!!' shouted Barry. All the squirrels sniggered and nudged each other.

'More, more,' they demanded. 'Show us how far you can spit.'

'Children!!' shouted the adult squirrels from the trees above.

'Skinny rats!!' Barry shouted after them as they all ran giggling after their parents.

The long grass was full of rotten apples that drew slugs from all over the garden. Barry got so fat he could hardly get into his kettle. The last of the golden leaves fell from the trees and the days grew shorter and darker. The other birds left the garden until there were only the sparrows and blackbirds left. Even the blue-tits had gone next door to eat peanuts.

Through October the air held on to the last warmth of summer but in November it grew colder with mornings crisp and frosty. Barry was too excited with his adventures to notice the weather. When his breath came out in little clouds he climbed into his kettle and blew up the spout.

'Tea's ready,' he shouted.

'Idiot,' said a sparrow.

'You've got no sense of humour,' said Barry. 'That's your trouble.'

It wasn't until January that the adventure began to wear thin. The frost stayed all day now. Up at the empty house with no one to light the fire the windows were covered with ice like lace curtains. In the cellar the rats shivered and thought about moving to another home. The worms went deep into the ground and next-door's cat was being fed in the house.

Barry shuffled around in the leaves finding fewer and fewer slugs. He began to lose weight and as he got thinner he lost his protection against the cold. At the bottom of his spines his fleas huddled together for warmth. He snuggled deep into his kettle and for the first time since autumn thought about his mother and his brothers and sisters. A lump came to his throat but his pride wouldn't let him go and curl up next to them under the warm shed.

'I'm staying awake all winter,' he said. But it was difficult to sound convincing with chattering teeth.

By February he was very thin and had a nasty cold that refused to go away. Every time the sun came out he thought that perhaps it was spring and that the others would soon come out from under the shed but the winter still had a long way to go and to prove it, it started to snow.

It began as he fell asleep and it snowed all night. Barry curled up as small as he could in his kettle but the cold went right through him. It crept down his spines like sharp needles. His paws had turned blue and hurt so much he could hardly move them. He knew now why hedgehogs hibernate. His tears ran cold down his face, turning to ice in the straw and making him even colder. His teeth chattered and his brain began to slide into a deep sleep.

With one great effort he pulled himself out of the kettle and went to look for the tunnel under the shed. But the snow had fallen so heavily that the entrance was buried and he couldn't find it. Round and round the shed he crawled getting weaker and weaker, until the greatest idea in the whole world seemed to be to curl up and go to sleep.

Sleep was wonderful. The snow grew warm as he faded away. He dreamt he was curled up in a nest of feathers with all his brothers and sisters. Then through the warmth, dark shapes appeared. Closer and closer they came, but Barry was so comfortable in the arms of death that he didn't see them.

'Hey, wake up,' said a voice.

'Come on,' said another, pushing him with a soft foot.

'Go away,' Barry heard himself mumble, but the voices kept pushing and poking him until he opened his eyes and unrolled.

Standing over him were Dave and Ernie, the two biggest rabbits in the garden. Barry suddenly felt afraid, but they were smiling down at him.

'Come on, young fellow. You can't sleep there. You'll be dead in no time at all,' said Dave.

'I can't find the way in,' said Barry, beginning to cry again.

'That's all right,' said Ernie. 'You come home with us.'

'But–' started Barry, remembering all the warnings his mother had given him about the rabbits.

'You'll die if you stay out here,' said Dave.

The two rabbits led the little hedgehog through the snowdrifts towards the warmth and safety of their underground home. Barry's feet were chapped and split from the cold and left little spots of blood on the snow. It seemed to take forever to reach the bottom of the garden.

As they dived down the tunnel into the rabbits' home the smell of fresh summer grass rose up to greet them. Deeper and deeper they went into the warren. On all sides of them there were more tunnels leading off into snug rooms where groups of rabbits peered out as they passed.

'Watcha got there, Ernie?' shouted a laughing voice. 'A pin-cushion?'

'Nah, he's brought Hilda a bag of nails,' called another.

At last they took a sharp turn left and came to a stop. Barry was so out of breath from keeping up with the long-legged rabbits that he couldn't speak. He certainly wasn't cold any more.

Ernie's wife Hilda and six young rabbits sat in the corner eating grass.

'Look what we found out in the snow,' said Ernie.

'Poor little mite,' said Hilda. 'He looks half-starved.'

Barry had been too cold and frightened to think

about it but he realised that he hadn't eaten anything for three days.

'Here, help yourself,' said the young rabbits, offering Barry their grass.

'I've never eaten grass,' said Barry. 'I don't think hedgehogs do.'

'Well, what do they eat?' asked Ernie.

'Slugs and worms and things like that.'

'Slugs?' chorused the young rabbits, 'how revolting.'

'Well yes, children,' said Hilda, 'It may seem revolting to us but it just so happens we're up to here with slugs and they're eating us out of house and home.'

'My goodness, you're right,' said Ernie. 'Wayne, Elvis, take our guest down to the larder.'

The two rabbits led Barry down deeper into the warren until they were far out under the river bed. They came to a huge cave piled high with grass and roots and leaves. Wherever he looked Barry could see thousands upon thousands of slugs. It was like a hundred Christmas dinners and three supermarkets rolled into one.

There were slugs of every size and colour from the tiny Mauve Mouthful to the wonderful succulent Brown Breakfast. There were slugs that Barry had heard about only in stories, like the Golden Gumdrop and the shining Great White Pudding. There were slugs that he had thought existed only in fairytales, like the exquisite Scarlet Slimebag that hedgehogs were supposed to have fought wars over. And lurking in the shadows like a vast beached whale, was the gigantically massively hugely enormous legendary Black Banquet. It rolled across the grass swallowing half a lawn a day and blowing out clouds of foul smelling steam. There seemed to be an endless variety of slugs and they were all for Barry.

The rabbits couldn't bear to watch as he dived into a pile of grass and began to eat. One by one they turned green and left the room.

'I don't know what they're so disgusted about,' thought Barry. 'At least I don't eat my food twice like they do.'

For the next three weeks Barry hardly left the larder. He ate and slept then ate some more and slept again. At first the young rabbits would hide in the tunnel giggling and daring each other to go and watch him eating but they all got used to it and he soon became friends with everyone.

'My mum and all the other animals say you're all crooks and dead common,' he said, 'but she's wrong.'

'We don't care,' said Ernie. 'Stops them bothering us.'

'She says you shout and swear all the time, but I think you're all great.'

'Well, we like to have a good time,' said Hilda.

'Rock and roll,' said Wayne.

'Yeah,' said Elvis.

March came and went and in early April Barry felt a breath of air from above ground tickle the back of his nose. Spring had arrived and was calling him.

Below the shed the other hedgehogs began to stir. Barry's mother rolled over and stretched. She reached out with her eyes still closed to where Barry should have been but the grass was cold and damp. At first she thought he might have got up early, but when she looked she could see that his bed hadn't been slept in at all.

She woke the others and they hurried out into the spring sunshine. Over a winter of hibernating they had grown thin and the sunlight blinded them after their long sleep of darkness.

'He's dead,' cried Barry's mother, 'I know he is. My poor little mite is frozen stiff and all alone.'

She snuffled around in the grass and bushes but there was no sign of him. She found his kettle but it was cold and empty.

'I blame myself,' said Barry's mother, 'I should never have left him.'

She raced round and round in circles looking for her son. There was no stopping her. The others tried to tell her she was wasting her time but she didn't hear them.

She ran in larger and larger circles until she was right out of the orchard and down near the bottom of the garden. She darted under bushes, looked deep into the pond, jumped over a rotten log and came crashing down on a big fat prickly mattress.

'Hello, Mum.'

'Barry?'

'Hello, Mum.'

'Barry, is it really you?'

'Yes, Mum.'

'I thought you were dead,' said his mother, hugging him the way only one hedgehog can hug another.

They went back to the shed and while all the others sat in a big circle he told them his story. It took two days to tell it because every time he started describing the wonderful slugs he had eaten everyone had to rush outside and find some food.

'Now then, young hedgehogs, just let that be a lesson to you all,' said a wise old grandfather.

'How do you mean, sir?' said Barry's little brother.

'Well, er, you tell them, Barry.'

'The moral of the story is that if you don't listen to your mother you could end up with lots of new friends and tons and tons of amazing slugs to eat.'

'BARRY!!'

'Sorry, Mum.'

The Boy Next Door

Elsie the mole had never felt so miserable in her life. She had a terrible headache and an awful cold and to make it worse she was in love with the boy next door who didn't even notice her.

She had caught the cold because she kept tunnelling up to next-door's lawn in the middle of winter. Down in the tunnels where she lived with her mother it was damp and warm, but up above there was a thick frost on the grass and dark grey clouds full of snow.

'It's your own fault,' said her mother, 'chasing round after that boy like that.'

'He doesn't even know I exist,' complained Elsie, sniffing loudly.

'Well, no nice mole would want someone who

rushes around like you do,' said her mother.

Elsie's heart-throb was different from all the other moles. He didn't live in dark tunnels like the rest of them. He was a brave and fearless adventurer who spent most of his life tightrope walking across the garden. He had a brother who was just the same and together they performed an amazing double act high above next-door's lawn. Sometimes one of them came down on to the lawn but Elsie was too nervous to speak and just peered out from the flower-beds with her little heart full of love.

The reason Elsie had a headache was because of her cold. Moles who spend most of their lives in dark tunnels don't need to see and so they are nearly blind. They find their way round with their noses but because Elsie had a cold she couldn't smell anything. Usually she could pick up a worm's sweat twenty metres away, but now she couldn't even smell her own armpits and kept crashing into everything. Every time the tunnel went left or right Elsie didn't. She went flying straight on into the wall and that was why she had a headache.

'Nobody loves me,' she wailed. 'I wish I were dead.'

'Why don't you just curl up in the nest and I'll bring you a nice hot slug?' suggested her mother but Elsie just couldn't sit still. Every time she closed her eyes she saw the boy next door and had to go rushing off down the tunnels to find him.

Her eyes were streaming and her head was throbbing and even though she could hardly see past the end of her nose, she could tell that her hero was not there. She was heartbroken and waddled back to her nest to cry herself to sleep. He wasn't there the next day or the next. In fact, it was over a week before Elsie saw him again. By then she had decided that she would never love anyone again and would spend the rest of her life stamping on earwigs and kicking worms.

After a week her cold was getting better and she decided to go next door one last time. The winter sun shone softly through the cold air and there across the lawn, dark and mysterious, was her great love. He was lying asleep in the grass all black and dull like rich velvet.

'It's now or never,' thought Elsie and tiptoed shyly out from the lavender bushes. She ran across the lawn towards her sweetheart who lay in a dark blur beneath the clothes-line. As she drew close, she tripped over a clothes-peg and landed right on top of him.

'Oh, my darling!' she cried, flinging her stubby little paws around the dark frostbitten shape.

'Oi,' said Neville the rat, who had been hiding behind a concrete gnome, 'that's my sock. I saw it first.'

Ethel the Chicken

Behind the house, at the bottom of the overgrown garden, in a wooden box hidden under a bramble bush, lived a chicken called Ethel. On the side of the box was a label that said 'FIRST CLASS ORANGES'. Even though chickens are nearly as stupid as sheep, Ethel knew that she was not an orange.

'I am a chicken,' she said.

'Prove it,' said a young rat called Neville, who lived in a paper bag nest under the old house. He was only a child and had never seen an orange or a chicken before.

'Wow, a talking chicken!' shouted an ant, but no one could hear her because she was very very small and before she could rush off and tell her four hundred and eighty brothers and sisters Ethel ate her.

'Listen, rat,' said Ethel, 'oranges are round and don't have feathers and don't lay eggs.'

'They might,' said Neville.

'You're a stupid little rat,' said Ethel, 'nearly as stupid as a sheep.' And she laid an egg.

'Is that an orange?' asked Neville.

'Of course not, it's an egg,' snapped Ethel.

'But it's round and got no feathers,' said Neville. Before Ethel could say anything else, Neville's mother came rushing down the lawn and grabbed him by the ear.

'How many times have I told you not to talk to strange fruit?' she said as she dragged him off.

Ethel settled back down on her nest and looked through the tall grass at the old house. It was a very long time since anyone had come out into the garden.

'It's probably an hour,' she thought to herself. The old lady who had lived in the house had gone away ages ago but chickens can't tell the time. She knew she hadn't been given any corn that morning but she'd had an enormous worm and a couple of lovely slugs for breakfast so she wasn't hungry.

When the old lady's nephews had come and taken all the furniture away they hadn't seen Ethel. They had come out into the back garden and folded up the deck-chairs but Ethel had heard them talking about chicken and chips and had sat very still under the rhubarb until they'd gone. They'd closed the curtains, locked the doors and driven off in a red car.

Ethel felt that there was more to life than eating worms and slugs and laying eggs, but she didn't know what it was. She tried to think about it but chickens' brains aren't very good at thinking and every time she tried she fell asleep. As she sat there dozing away in the afternoon sunshine, young Neville came back.

'My mum says I've got to come and say sorry for being cheeky to you,' he said. Ethel said it was all right and that she was sure he was quite a good boy really. 'Can I be your friend?' asked Neville.

'Of course you can,' said the old hen, and they chatted about this and that for a while. Neville said his mum had been in a bad mood ever since the old lady had gone.

'We used to eat cake and toffees,' he explained, 'but now the house is empty we have to eat woodlice all the time.'

'I like woodlice,' said Ethel. But then, she had never eaten cake.

'I don't,' said Neville. 'All the bits stick in your teeth.'

'I haven't got teeth,' Ethel told him. 'I like the way their legs tickle as you swallow them.'

Neville looked a bit green at this and said he had to go and help his dad chew up some paper bags. Ethel told him to come and see her any time he felt like it. When he had gone she realised what the other thing was that she had been trying to think of. It was loneliness.

Since the old lady had gone, no one had come to see her. Every morning the old lady had come down the garden with a mug of corn and every morning she had tickled the top of Ethel's head and talked to her. Most of the time Ethel hadn't been able to understand what the old lady had been talking about but the words had always felt warm and comforting in her ears. Ethel was old herself and hardly ever laid an egg but the old lady had never seemed to mind.

It was only now that the young rat had started to visit her that she realised how much she missed the old lady and how lonely she was. The hedgehogs who came and took the occasional egg she rolled out of her box were a miserable lot. You couldn't talk to them at all. When Ethel tried they just grunted a bit and shuffled off into the undergrowth. The other birds laughed at her because she was big and lumpy and couldn't fly and next-door's cat just sneered at her. But then next-door's cat sneered at everybody.

The next day young Neville came to see Ethel again. He told her about all sorts of wonderful things she had never heard of like skateboards and calculators. But when Ethel tried to talk about slugs, Neville grew restless and sat there fidgeting and sucking bits of woodlouse out of his teeth. Eventually he wandered off saying he had to help his dad again.

It was a lovely hot summer afternoon. Ethel sank into her nest, half asleep, and clucked softly to herself. Bright butterflies skipped in and out of the dandelion flowers whistling the latest tune. Ethel had never eaten a butterfly and wondered what they tasted like. She didn't know that they were just caterpillars with their best clothes on.

She could hear children playing in the garden next door. She liked children. The old lady had brought some to see her once and they'd all tickled her feathers and cuddled her. It had made her feel very happy.

She thought about going next door to see the children but there was a big hedge and a tall fence all round the garden, far too tall for a fat old chicken to get over. At her age, it was all she could do to jump up on to the roof of her box. A diet of juicy worms and slugs had made her so fat that sometimes as she waddled around the lawn, she tripped over her own feet. It was no fun being old and even worse being lonely and old.

'You ought to try and get out a bit more,' said Neville's mum, when Ethel said she felt lonely. 'There's all sorts of things going on round the garden.'

'I'm too old for all that,' said Ethel. 'All I want is my old lady to come back.'

'You should go and meet the rabbits down by the apple trees,' Neville's mum went on, but there was no cheering Ethel up.

'I just want it to be like it used to be,' she said sadly.

The summer drifted lazily on. Neville came to see Ethel less and less. He wanted to play with his friends, to chase squirrels and tease next-door's cat, not listen to an old chicken talk about slugs. Neville's mother didn't come any more either, not now she had seven new children to look after. Ethel couldn't blame them, she knew she was boring. Sometimes just the simple effort of looking for worms seemed too much. In the good old days there had always been a magic in scratching away at the earth and jumping back, head to one side, to find some new treasure. Now everything seemed to have lost its taste. Grass, worms, daffodils or slugs, it was all the same. Only woodlice had any sweetness left and they seemed to run faster than they used to and be harder to catch.

The first leaves began to fall and a breath of cold crept into the garden. The children next door stopped playing outside and the air was filled with the thick smoke of autumn as everybody piled up the dying plants into smouldering bonfires. In Ethel's garden the dead flowers shrivelled up with no one to clear them away. They hung over like thin skeletons and in the mornings were stiff with frost. The golden leaves turned brown and collected in damp piles on the lawn. The days grew dark and short as winter covered the world. Ethel hid deep in her straw and tried to sleep. The slugs had finished and the worms had gone deeper into the earth. A few spiders still survived the cold and it was those that kept her going.

Rain came and broke up the old flowers and washed them into the ground. It washed the label off Ethel's box and dripped in through the cracks in the wood. It ran down her face so that if you had seen her you would have said you'd seen a chicken cry. The dampness crept into her bones and made them creak and her loneliness seemed to grow as dark as the winter nights.

She cheered up a bit when the snow came. It made the garden bright and clean. It covered her box with a thick coat that kept her warm and dry and it lasted for weeks. Neville began to visit her again and although Ethel knew he was only coming to get away from his baby brothers and sisters, she was glad to see him. He made a tunnel under the snow right across the lawn and sat shivering in front of Ethel's box telling her all his news.

'My dad's been eaten by next-door's cat,' he said, through chattering teeth, 'and my brother Trevor.'

Ethel couldn't think of anything to say so she tucked the young rat up in the straw next to her and clucked. It started to snow again, great big flakes that seemed to float around for ages before they landed.

'Why's it so cold?' said Neville, who had never seen a winter before.

'I don't know,' said Ethel. 'It always seems to be cold when it snows.'

'Is it going to be like this forever?' he asked.

'Oh no, it always goes away again,' said Ethel.

'What, back up in the sky?'

'I don't think so.'

'Well, where does it go?' asked Neville.

'I don't know,' she replied.

Neville's little sister, Tracy, popped up out of the tunnel and jumped up and down in front of them blowing out white puffs of cold breath.

'Mum says you've got to come home,' she squeaked. 'We've run out of paper bags.'

Neville climbed out of the warm and followed his little sister back down the tunnel. Ethel closed her eyes and dreamt of the old lady surrounded by sunshine and fresh grass.

The snow melted, more rain came and went and then one day the air seemed to be a little warmer. The sun grew bigger and stayed in the sky longer each day and opened new buds on the sleeping trees. Ethel got up and scratched about on the lawn. She found herself wandering further and further from her box into corners of the garden she had long forgotten. The rheumatism in her bones seemed to fade until she could no longer hear her joints creaking. She fluttered right up into an old apple tree and sat there feeling quite pleased with herself.

As she sat there fluffing her feathers out, one of the curtains at the back of the house opened and a man looked out. She kept very still. One by one all the curtains were opened, windows and doors too. Ethel kept so still that her legs went to sleep and she fell out of the tree. She lay in the grass but no one came. No one had seen her and after a while the man shut the doors and windows and went away.

Later on Neville slipped out of the shadows and jumped into Ethel's box.

'I'm not happy,' he said, sounding quite grown up. 'Humans and rats are not friends.'

'Don't be silly,' said Ethel. 'The old lady was wonderful.'

'She was old,' said Neville. 'She didn't know we were there. Most people don't like us and try and kill us.'

'What on earth for?' asked Ethel.

'My mum says it's because we chew their slippers,' said Neville.

Ethel didn't know what slippers where and when Neville told her she got that horrid taste in her mouth you get when someone sucks a handkerchief. She said she was sure he was wrong and anyway perhaps the old lady was coming back. But she didn't. Over the next few weeks the man brought lots of people to the house but none of them was the old lady. Ethel sat quietly in her box and no one saw her. She knew in her heart that the young rat was probably right and she grew nervous at all the coming and going.

A few days later Neville and his mother came to say goodbye.

'We're going to live in this wonderful drain with my brother,' said Neville, all excited. 'It goes right under the best restaurant in town. The rubbish is really great.'

Ethel felt very sad when they had gone. She even ignored a giant slug that slithered right in front of her box.

One day some people came to the house and stayed. They took down all the old grey curtains and put up new ones covered in big red flowers. At night the windows were filled with yellow light that poured out on to the lawn. New smells drifted down the garden, wonderful warm smells that Ethel had never experienced before. There was still no sign of the old lady. A man came out on Saturday and cut the grass. He passed right by Ethel hiding in the back of her box, but he never saw her.

Then as if by magic there were children in the garden. A boy and a girl running and laughing, climbing the trees and swinging from the branches. Round and round they ran throwing a big blue ball in the air. A big blue ball which bounced and rolled and rolled and rolled right up to Ethel's box.

'Look, look, look,' shouted the little girl to her brother. They reached out and tickled Ethel in exactly the right place. She shut her eyes and felt all her loneliness slip away.

The little girl tucked Ethel under her arm and carried her up to the house. The little boy ran beside her smiling and laughing.

Later on, the man gave Ethel a smart new box with a label on the side that said 'BEST APPLES'. 'I am a chicken,' said Ethel to herself as she settled down into her wonderful new straw.

'And I shall call you Doris,' said the little girl as she poured her out a mug of corn.

Also available from Hodder Children's Books:

Attila the Bluebottle by Colin Thompson

Waking Up

At the end of a quiet street at the edge of a large town, between tidy houses and tidy gardens, was a wild place. Once it had been a garden like those on either side with a neat lawn and straight rows of flowers, but some years before, the old lady who had lived there had moved away and since then the garden had become a dark and mysterious jungle. In the middle of this wild place was an empty house, called fourteen, that was slowly disappearing behind crawling bushes and overgrown trees.

As time passed the grass grew taller burying the path from the front gate, the ivy crawled up the walls and slipped in through the broken windows. The trees wove new branches together and the garden became a closed and secret place.

In the jungle the honeysuckle filled the air with heavy dreams, and animals that had nowhere else to go made their homes in its welcoming branches and secret places. Moles and rats that had been driven from the tidy gardens all around took refuge there. Beyond the edge of the abandoned lawn under a thick bramble bush a chicken lived in an orange box, and up on the roof of the house crows had filled the chimneys with years of nests. Rabbits that could never find enough to eat anywhere else lived in a wild warren at the bottom of the garden beneath a crowded hedge. Beyond the hedge through brambles and giant hogweed taller than men a dusty towpath ran beside an old canal and across the canal was a desperate place of crumbling factories and fractured concrete.

The years passed and then one day as spring began to push the winter aside the old lady's nephew lifted away the broken gate and took his family to live in the neglected house.

Windows stiff with age were forced open and given new panes of glass and a coat of paint. The branches that had grown across them were chopped down and sunshine crept into the house for the first time in years. As the rooms grew warm again the dampness that had reached up to the highest ceilings was driven back into the earth.

In three quick weeks, the cobwebs were swept away, the holes that had let the rats in were filled up and the crows' nests were pushed out of the chimneys with stiff brushes.

When the chimneys were clear they lit fires in every room. The chopped down branches cracked as the flames ate through them and filled the air with sweet smelling smoke. The thin shoots of plants that had crept into the house behind the plaster shrivelled away and in a few days it was as if they had never been there. Once again the house was back in human hands.

Out in the garden the air was filled with nervous talk as the animals sat and waited. The homeless crows huddled in the tall trees and made everyone else miserable. Eventually they made new nests in the high branches but for months afterwards they complained to anyone who would listen.

'Just wait,' they said, 'When they've finished with the house, they'll come out here and kill the garden.'

The other animals said nothing because they were all frightened that what the crows were saying might be true.

'Of course, they'll wait until we've built new nests,' said the crows. 'They'll wait 'till we're all nicely settled in with fresh eggs ready to hatch, then they'll come out and chop everything down until it's as flat and dead as all the other gardens.'

It looked as though the crows were right, for as spring turned into early summer the man bought a bright red lawnmower and attacked the back garden. The machine flew over the grass like an eagle, tearing it to pieces as it passed. The green tunnels that the mice had made over the years vanished in a minute, leaving a wide open yellow space that was unsafe to cross. From her box under the bush Ethel the chicken sat very still and watched him go by. From the tops of the trees the crows looked down too scared of the man to go and pick up the worms he had disturbed. All the terrible things they had predicted were coming true.

Every weekend the family pulled out the weeds that had grown around the house and swept up the dead leaves. They cut back the ivy until it was no taller than a dog and piled everything up into a huge bonfire in the old vegetable garden.

In the evenings as the days grew longer the man sat in an armchair by the French windows, gazed out across the tidy lawn at the dense undergrowth beyond and fell asleep. Sometimes he would wake up just as the light was fading away and see the rabbits and hedgehogs moving softly in the shadows. Sometimes he would see the blackbirds hopping across the grass and other birds flying in from all around to roost in the tall trees. Maybe something told him that if he cut everything down they would all go away, or maybe he was just lazy, but as the summer grew warmer his enthusiasm for gardening grew less and less.

The animals grew more and more restless. They knew the people would chop everything down. That's what people did, they only had to look at every other garden to see that. But the family finished playing with their bonfire and then left everything alone. Some of the smaller more nervous animals like the voles and the shrews moved out into the narrow strip of wasteland by the canal, but for most of them there was nowhere else to go and they just had to watch and wait.

'They're just biding their time,' said the crows.

'What for?' asked Ethel the chicken, but no one knew.

And then something happened that made the family make up its mind once and for all.